FIRST GRADE TAKES A TEST

Miriam Cohen

Illustrated by Lillian Hoban

A Young Yearling Book

Published by
Dell Publishing
a division of
Bantam Doubleday Dell Publishing Group, Inc.
1540 Broadway
New York, New York 10036

The trademark Yearling ® is registered in the U.S. Patent
and Trademark Office.

The trademark Dell® is registered in the U.S. Patent and Trademark
Office.

ISBN: 0-440-42500-X
Reprinted by arrangement with Greenwillow Books, a division
of William Morrow & Company, Inc.

Printed in the United States of America

November 1983
20 19 18 17 16 15 14
WES

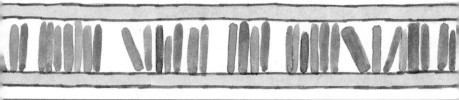

"No," said Anna Maria. "I told them I had to come back. I told them first grade needs me."
"It's good to be together again,"
said the teacher.
"We don't need a test to tell us that!"

"Aren't you in the special class anymore?" everyone asked.

And on Friday, when the first grade came
running into their room, Anna Maria
was sitting in the rocking chair.

On Wednesday she told Sara,
"Margaret doesn't know
how to help George with
his arithmetic."

On Thursday she
whispered something
to the teacher.

Every day, Anna Maria went to the special class. But first thing each morning she peeked into first grade to tell them things. On Monday she said, "Don't forget to water the plants."

On Tuesday she asked, "Who is reminding the teacher when it is time to pass out the papers?"

Margaret helped George
with his arithmetic.
By the time the bell rang,
everyone felt a lot better.

Everybody went back to work. Jim and Paul started fixing their undersea racing car. Sara sat in the rocker reading a good book called *Worms: Our Friends in the Earth.*

Jim said, "Let's weigh them!"
They rushed to the scale.
Both cookies weighed the same!
"Good thinking, Jim!" said the teacher.

"Let me see!" They all looked at Sara's
and Danny's cookies and felt them.
But nobody could tell which was bigger.

When Danny got his, he yelled,
"Sara got a fatter cookie than I did!"
"Mine is fatter, but yours is wider,"
Sara said.

Everybody was quiet.
Then the teacher
brought out cookies
she had made.

You can build things! You can read books!
You can make pictures! You have good ideas!
And another thing. The test doesn't tell you
if you are a kind person who helps your friend.
Those are important things.''

"Listen to me!" They had never
heard their teacher sound like that.
"The test doesn't tell everything.
It doesn't tell all the things
you *can* do!

Paul was mad. He said to Danny,
"*You're* not going with Anna Maria, dummy!"
"You're a dummy!" Danny said.
Everybody began calling someone else
"Dummy! Dummy!"
Jim whispered it to himself. "Dummy!"

When Margaret came back from getting a drink of water, she told everybody, "Anna Maria is in the special class because she did a good test!" Everyone looked around the room.

One day, after they had almost forgotten the test,
the lady from the principal's office came back.
She said to Anna Maria,
"Come with me, dear."
And they went away down the hall.

"Ooh," Sara said, "I *know* I did it wrong!"
"Don't worry," Jim said.
"You're as smart as I am."

Anna Maria was smiling and telling everyone,
"That was *easy*."

Suddenly the teacher said, "The time is up!"
"I'm not finished!" cried everyone except
Anna Maria. But the teacher had to take
the tests away.

Jim wondered what being tall had to do with getting a baloney sandwich. And was it really a *baloney* sandwich? It might be tomato. . . . Jim took a long time on that one.

On the test there was a picture of Sally and Tom.
Sally was giving Tom something. It looked like
a baloney sandwich. Underneath it said:

Sally is taller than Tom. ☐
Tom is taller than Sally. ☐

He poked Willy. "Firemen get your head out when it's stuck," he said. "My uncle had his head stuck in a big pipe, and the firemen came and got it out."
But none of the boxes said that.

Sammy read:

What do firemen do?

make bread ☐
put out fires ☐
sing ☐

"Rabbits have to eat carrots,
or their teeth will get too long
and stick into them," he said.
The teacher nodded and smiled,
but she put her finger to her lips.
George carefully drew in a carrot
so the test people would know.

George looked at the test. It said:

Rabbits eat
☐ lettuce ☐ dog food
☐ sandwiches

He raised his hand.

You must work quickly.
But do not worry—
you can do it.
Ready! Begin!"

Their teacher told first grade how to do
the test. She said, "Read the questions
carefully. Then take your pencil and
fill in the box next to the right answer.

She smiled at the first grade.
"We have some tests for you," she said.
"Oh, good," said Anna Maria.
"Now we can find out how smart we are."

A lady from the principal's office
came to the first grade.
She had a big pile of papers with
little boxes all over them.

For Monroe who gave me the idea,
and for David who has lots of good ideas

With thanks to the North Dakota Study Group
on Evaluation—especially to Lillian Weber,
Deborah Meier, Ann Cook, and Vito Perrone